Love In Transit

Pag-yel Taglan Rutherford

Published by Pag-yel Taglan Rutherford, 2024.

This is a work of fiction. Similarities to real people, places, or events are entirely coincidental.

LOVE IN TRANSIT

First edition. October 22, 2024.

Copyright © 2024 Pag-yel Taglan Rutherford.

ISBN: 979-8227235992

Written by Pag-yel Taglan Rutherford.

Table of Contents

LOVE IN TRANSIT 1
INTRODUCTION 3
CHAPTER 1 6
CHAPTER 2 13
CHAPTER 3 22
CHAPTER 4 30
CHAPTER 5 34
CHAPTER 6 38
CHAPTER 7 41
CHAPTER 8 46
CHAPTER 9 52
CHAPTER 10 | EPILOGUE 58

LOVE IN TRANSIT

INTRODUCTION
   CHAPTER 1
   1.1 Emily's life before
   CHAPTER 2
   2.1 How Emily's relationship with her father influences her behavior
   2.2 How Emily's father's death affects her mental state
   2.3 How Emily's denial of her father's death affect her interactions with the townspeople
   CHAPTER 3
   3.1 The long-term consequences of Emily's codependency with her father
   3.2 How Emily's codependency with her father affects her independence
   CHAPTER 4
   4.1 Emily's sense of identity changed after her father's death
   CHAPTER 5
   5.1 How Emily's grief manifests in her daily life
   CHAPTER 6
   6.1 "Departure" - Emily boards the train, leaving her stressful life behind.
   6.2 "Unexpected Encounter" - Emily meets Ryan, a charming traveler.
   6.3 "Small Talk" - Emily and Ryan strike up a conversation.
   6.4 "City Lights" - The train arrives in Chicago; Emily and Ryan explore.
   6.5 "Dinner with Strangers" - Emily and Ryan share a romantic dinner.
   write this chapter in full detail.
   CHAPTER 7
   7.1 "Train Tales" - Ryan shares stories of his travels.

7.2 "Business and Pleasure" - Emily struggles to balance work and leisure.

7.3 "Shared Laughter" - Emily and Ryan bond over humor.

7.4 "Midnight Conversations" - Deep conversations under starry skies.

7.5 "Crossing State Lines" - The train enters the Rocky Mountains.

CHAPTER 8

8.1 "Past Encounters" - Emily's past relationships haunt her.

8.2 "Ryan's Secrets" - Ryan's mysterious past surfaces.

8.3 "Train Delay" - The train breaks down; tensions rise.

8.4 "Stormy Weather" - Emily and Ryan face challenges amid a storm.

8.5 "Fear of Commitment" - Emily's doubts about love resurface.

CHAPTER 9

9.1 "Heart-to-Heart" - Emily and Ryan confront their fears.

9.2 "New Beginnings" - Emily and Ryan decide on a future.

9.3 "Last Stop" - The train reaches its final destination.

9.4 "Bittersweet Goodbye" - Emily and Ryan face separation.

9.5 "Love on Track" - Emily and Ryan reunite, embracing their love.

CHAPTER 10

5.1 Epilogue

INTRODUCTION

The rhythmic clatter of train wheels against the tracks echoed through the compartment, a soothing symphony that wrapped around Emily and Ryan like a warm embrace. Sunlight streamed through the large windows, casting golden rays that danced across their faces, illuminating the joy that radiated from them. Outside, the landscape morphed into a blur of vibrant greens and browns, punctuated by the occasional flash of wildflowers swaying in the gentle breeze. It was a picturesque backdrop for their journey—a journey that had begun as a mere escape from reality but had blossomed into something infinitely more profound.

As they sat side by side, Emily felt a sense of comfort wash over her. Each time she glanced at Ryan, she was reminded of how effortlessly they connected. His tousled hair caught the light just right, framing his face in a way that made her heart flutter. He turned to her, his eyes sparkling with mischief and warmth, and she couldn't help but smile back. It was moments like these that made her realize how transformative love could be—how it could turn an ordinary train ride into an extraordinary adventure.

"Where to next?" Ryan asked playfully, leaning closer as if sharing a secret. The question hung in the air, filled with promise and spontaneity. Emily loved this about him; he had a way of making every moment feel alive with possibility. She considered their options—each destination holding its own allure and adventure.

"Let's go somewhere we've never been before," she suggested, her voice brimming with excitement. "Somewhere we can explore together." Ryan nodded enthusiastically, his eyes lighting up at the thought. They began brainstorming potential destinations—cities filled with culture, nature trails waiting to be hiked, and hidden gems waiting to be discovered.

As they plotted their next adventure, Emily felt a thrill coursing through her veins. This was what life was about—embracing spontaneity and living in the moment. With Ryan by her side, she felt empowered to step outside her comfort zone and embrace whatever came their way.

The train continued its journey through breathtaking landscapes—majestic mountains rising in the distance and valleys stretching wide beneath them. Each view outside seemed to mirror the emotional landscapes they were traversing together: beautiful, complex, and filled with uncharted territory. They shared stories and laughter as they traveled deeper into each other's lives, peeling back layers of vulnerability that had once held them back.

As dusk began to settle over the horizon, painting the sky in hues of orange and purple, Emily felt an overwhelming sense of gratitude for this journey they were on—not just for the places they explored but for the connection they had forged. Their hearts were intertwined like the train tracks stretching endlessly before them—a promise of continuity and adventure.

"Do you remember our first night together?" Ryan asked suddenly, breaking into her thoughts. His voice was soft yet filled with nostalgia. "Under those stars in Rocky Mountain National Park?"

Emily smiled at the memory—the way they had shared secrets and dreams beneath a blanket of stars that seemed to echo their hopes for the future. "How could I forget? It felt like time stood still," she replied, her heart swelling at the recollection.

Ryan turned serious for a moment; his gaze locked onto hers with an intensity that made her breath catch. "That night changed everything for me," he confessed. "I realized how rare it is to find someone who understands you so deeply."

Her heart raced at his words; it was as if he had peeled back another layer of their connection—exposing raw emotions that lay beneath the surface. "I feel the same way," she admitted softly. "You've shown me that love doesn't have to be scary; it can be beautiful."

With those words hanging between them like a fragile thread connecting their hearts, Ryan reached for her hand—a simple gesture that spoke volumes about their commitment to one another. The warmth of his touch sent shivers down Emily's spine; it was grounding yet exhilarating all at once.

As they rode deeper into the night, surrounded by darkness punctuated only by twinkling lights from distant towns passing by, Emily found herself reflecting on how far they had come since that fateful day on the train when their paths first crossed. They had navigated fears and insecurities together—facing past heartbreaks while embracing new beginnings filled with hope.

In this moment of quiet intimacy aboard the train—a vessel carrying them toward new adventures—Emily realized how much she cherished not just Ryan's presence but also what he represented: freedom from fear, acceptance of vulnerability, and an unwavering belief in love's power to heal.

As they approached their next destination—a city alive with possibilities—Emily felt a rush of excitement course through her veins once more; this was not just another stop along their journey but rather another chapter waiting to unfold in their story together.

"Forever in transit," Ryan said suddenly as if reading her thoughts aloud—a phrase that encapsulated everything they had built together thus far: an unending journey marked by love and exploration.

Emily smiled brightly at him; she knew deep down that no matter where life took them next—whether across oceans or simply down familiar streets—they would face it hand in hand—two souls forever intertwined amidst life's beautiful chaos.

With hearts full of hope and excitement for what lay ahead, they leaned back against each other as the train continued onward—ready for whatever adventures awaited them on this beautiful journey called life—a journey defined not merely by destinations but by love shared along each winding track leading toward endless possibilities yet unseen.

CHAPTER 1

Emily stood at the threshold of her home, a place that had once been a sanctuary but had slowly morphed into a prison of her own making. The walls seemed to close in on her, echoing the weight of unfulfilled expectations and relentless responsibilities. It was a life filled with deadlines, meetings, and the constant hum of anxiety that gnawed at her peace of mind. Each day felt like a monotonous cycle, where the vibrant colors of her dreams faded into dull grays. She could no longer ignore the growing sense of suffocation that enveloped her.

The catalyst for her decision to leave came unexpectedly during a particularly grueling week at work. Emily had poured herself into a project that seemed to consume every ounce of energy she possessed. Late nights blurred into early mornings, and the thrill of accomplishment was overshadowed by the exhaustion that followed. When she finally presented her work to her team, it was met with lukewarm applause rather than the enthusiastic praise she had hoped for. The disappointment settled heavily in her chest, igniting a spark of rebellion against the life she had built.

That evening, as she sat alone in her dimly lit living room, Emily scrolled through photos from past travels—memories filled with laughter and adventure. Each image was a reminder of who she used to be: carefree, spontaneous, and full of life. The realization hit her like a thunderbolt: she had allowed the pressures of adulthood to extinguish that vibrant spirit. In that moment, she made a choice—a decision to reclaim her joy and rediscover herself beyond the confines of her career.

The next day, Emily packed a small bag with essentials, leaving behind the weighty expectations that had tethered her to a life she no longer recognized. She felt an exhilarating rush as she boarded the train bound for Chicago—a city that promised new experiences and perhaps even new friendships. As the train pulled away from the station, she glanced back at her old life fading into the distance, feeling an overwhelming sense of liberation.

It was on this journey that she would meet Ryan—a charming traveler whose presence would further ignite the spark within her. Their unexpected encounter began with small talk, but it quickly blossomed into something deeper as they shared stories and laughter. Ryan's adventurous spirit mirrored Emily's long-buried desires, and for the first time in years, she felt alive again.

As they explored Chicago together—the city lights twinkling like stars against the night sky—Emily realized how much she had missed these simple pleasures. They wandered through bustling streets filled with street performers and tantalizing aromas from food vendors. The vibrancy of the city matched the excitement bubbling within her; it was as if every corner held a new adventure waiting to unfold.

Their romantic dinner marked another turning point in Emily's journey. Over candlelight and shared dishes, they delved into conversations about their lives—dreams, fears, and aspirations laid bare between them. Emily found herself opening up in ways she hadn't anticipated; Ryan listened intently, offering encouragement and understanding without judgment. In his presence, she felt safe to explore not only who she was but who she wanted to become.

As their connection deepened over shared laughter and intimate moments, Emily began to confront the fears that had held her back for so long. She spoke candidly about her struggles with self-doubt and the pressure to succeed professionally while maintaining personal happiness. Ryan reciprocated with his vulnerabilities—his fear of commitment and losing his sense of adventure resonated deeply with her.

With each passing day in Chicago, Emily shed layers of insecurity that had accumulated over time. The city became a backdrop for healing; it reminded her that life was meant to be lived fully—not just endured. Ryan's presence encouraged her to embrace spontaneity once more; they ventured into new neighborhoods, tried unfamiliar foods, and danced under the stars as if no one were watching.

Yet even amidst this newfound freedom, Emily grappled with lingering doubts about returning home. Would she fall back into old patterns? Would the pressures of work once again overshadow her desire for adventure? But as each moment unfolded—each laugh shared and each story exchanged—she felt more certain about what lay ahead.

As their time together drew to a close, Emily faced the bittersweet reality of separation from Ryan—a connection that had blossomed so quickly yet felt so profound. They exchanged promises to stay in touch and plans for future adventures; it was a commitment forged not just in words but in shared experiences that would linger long after they parted ways.

Returning home after their whirlwind trip felt surreal; Emily stepped back into her familiar surroundings but with a renewed perspective on life. She realized that while challenges would always exist—both personally and professionally—she now possessed tools to navigate them with grace and courage.

Inspired by her journey with Ryan, Emily began making changes in her daily routine—setting aside time for self-care and pursuing hobbies that ignited joy within her soul. She reconnected with friends who shared similar passions for travel and adventure; together they planned weekend getaways filled with laughter and exploration.

In embracing spontaneity once more, Emily discovered hidden gems within her city—a quaint café tucked away on a side street or an art exhibit showcasing local talent. Each experience reminded her that adventure wasn't solely defined by far-flung destinations; it could also be found in everyday moments filled with curiosity and wonder.

As weeks turned into months after they departed from Chicago, Emily continued communicating regularly with Ryan—texting about their lives while reminiscing about their shared adventures. Their bond deepened despite physical distance; they encouraged one another through challenges while celebrating successes together.

Eventually, they made plans for another reunion—this time not just as travelers but as partners embarking on new adventures side by side. The anticipation built within Emily as she prepared for their next journey together—a testament to how far she had come since boarding that train bound for Chicago.

In reflecting on what had brought her here—the decision to leave behind stressors at home—Emily recognized it wasn't merely about escaping; it was about reclaiming herself amidst chaos. Travel had become more than just an escape; it represented growth—a powerful reminder that life could be lived fully when one embraced change rather than shying away from it.

As she boarded yet another train—this time alongside Ryan—Emily felt an exhilarating rush course through her veins once more; this journey would lead them toward new horizons filled with endless possibilities waiting patiently ahead on tracks leading toward love intertwined amidst every winding path yet unseen.

With hearts open wide ready for whatever lay ahead—Emily knew deep down this was just the beginning—a beautiful chapter unfolding before them both marked by adventure friendship love all intertwined forevermore along this remarkable journey called life together hand-in-hand navigating each twist turn along every track laid out before them both waiting patiently ahead beckoning them onward toward brighter tomorrows filled with hope joy laughter love all waiting just around each bend yet unseen ahead!

Before Emily decided to leave her life behind and embark on a journey of self-discovery, her existence was defined by isolation and suffocating expectations. Living in a once-grand but now decaying home, Emily was the last remnant of a proud Southern family, a woman trapped in the shadows of her father's authoritarian grip. Her father, Mr. Grierson, had been both her protector and her jailer, enforcing strict rules that kept her from forming relationships or pursuing her own happiness. He believed no man was good enough for his daughter, effectively isolating her from potential suitors and friends alike.

After the death of her father, Emily found herself grappling with profound loneliness. The man who had dominated her life was gone, leaving behind a void that she struggled to fill. For days, she refused to acknowledge his death, keeping his corpse in the house as if clinging to the last vestiges of control he had exerted over her. This denial was not just a reflection of grief; it was an indication of how deeply intertwined their lives had been. The townspeople watched with pity and concern as she descended further into isolation.

Emily's home became a symbol of her mental state—once vibrant and full of life, it had fallen into disrepair, mirroring the decay of her spirit. The heavy air inside was thick with dust and neglect, and the once-white walls bore witness to years of emotional turmoil. Tobe, her loyal servant, was the only person who moved about the house, bringing groceries and supplies while remaining a silent observer of Emily's unraveling life.

Over time, Emily became a recluse, rarely venturing outside or allowing anyone into her home. The townspeople regarded her as a "hereditary obligation," someone whose presence they tolerated out of respect for her family's history rather than genuine connection. Gossip surrounded Emily like a shroud; whispers about her eccentric behavior filled the air as they speculated about the strange smells emanating from her property and the peculiar choices she made.

Despite being surrounded by people, Emily felt utterly alone. The few interactions she had were often tinged with awkwardness and misunderstanding. When she attempted to engage with the community—like when she taught art lessons to local children—her efforts felt forced and unfulfilling. She longed for companionship but found herself trapped in a cycle of despair that left little room for joy or connection.

LOVE IN TRANSIT 11

The turning point came when she met Homer Barron, a laborer from the North who arrived in town after Mr. Grierson's death. Their relationship sparked intrigue among the townspeople; it was both scandalous and refreshing to see Emily engaging with someone outside her social class. For the first time in years, she felt a flicker of hope—a chance at happiness that seemed both exhilarating and terrifying.

However, as their courtship progressed, Emily's insecurities resurfaced. She feared losing Homer just as she had lost her father. The pressure to conform to societal expectations weighed heavily on her; she felt like an outsider in both love and life. When Homer disappeared from her life without explanation, it sent Emily spiraling back into despair—a familiar darkness that threatened to engulf her once more.

In an attempt to regain control over her life, Emily made choices that shocked those around her. She purchased arsenic under mysterious circumstances—an act that fueled rumors about potential self-harm or even worse intentions toward Homer. Yet these actions were less about malice and more about desperation—a cry for help masked by stubborn pride.

As time passed without resolution or closure regarding Homer's fate, Emily retreated further into herself. She locked away not only physical possessions but also emotional connections—choosing solitude over vulnerability. The house became a tomb for memories both cherished and haunting; it was where she kept Homer's presence alive long after his physical absence.

Emily's decision to leave all this behind came not from a place of recklessness but rather from an overwhelming desire for liberation. She recognized that staying within those walls would only lead to further decay—both of herself and the remnants of what had once been a vibrant life filled with hope and possibility.

The moment she boarded that train marked not just a departure from her physical surroundings but also an emotional release from years of pent-up sorrow and regret. It was an act of defiance against the expectations that had shackled her for so long—a bold step toward reclaiming agency over her narrative.

In meeting Ryan on that train, Emily discovered not just companionship but also kindred spirits who understood the complexities of fear and longing. Their conversations opened doors within her heart that had long been sealed shut; they allowed space for laughter amidst tears—a reminder that joy could coexist with pain.

As they explored Chicago together—the city lights illuminating their path—Emily felt herself awakening to possibilities previously thought lost forever. Each shared experience became a stepping stone toward healing; every moment spent together served as affirmation that life could be beautiful again.

Through Ryan's eyes, Emily began to see herself anew—not just as Miss Grierson burdened by family legacy but as a woman capable of forging her own destiny outside societal constraints. It was liberating to embrace spontaneity once more—to dance under stars without fear or judgment.

Ultimately, Emily's decision to leave behind everything familiar marked not just an escape but also an embrace of hope—a belief that love could flourish even amidst chaos if one dared to take risks along this unpredictable journey called life.

In leaving behind the weighty expectations tied to her past identity—both familial and societal—Emily embarked upon an adventure filled with uncertainty yet brimming with potential for growth transformation healing love all intertwined beautifully along this remarkable path ahead!

CHAPTER 2

How Emily's relationship with her father influence her behavior

Emily's relationship with her father profoundly shaped her behavior and personality throughout her life. Mr. Grierson, a wealthy and controlling figure, exerted an overwhelming influence on Emily, dictating not only her social interactions but also her emotional development. His overprotective nature left Emily isolated from the outside world, preventing her from forming meaningful connections with others and leading to a deep emotional dependence on him.

From a young age, Emily was subjected to her father's authoritarian control, which manifested in various ways. He believed that no man was good enough for his daughter, effectively driving away any potential suitors. This isolation stunted Emily's social skills and left her unprepared for adult relationships. The townspeople observed this dynamic, often picturing Emily as a fragile figure overshadowed by her father's imposing presence. Mr. Grierson's territorial nature made it clear that he viewed Emily as his possession rather than as an independent individual.

The impact of this relationship became even more pronounced after Mr. Grierson's death. Unable to cope with the loss of the only person who had been a constant in her life, Emily entered a state of denial, refusing to acknowledge his passing for three days. This behavior highlighted her deep-seated dependency on him and her inability to confront the reality of her situation. The isolation she experienced during her father's life continued after his death, as she withdrew further into herself and her decaying home.

Emily's emotional well-being was further compromised by the false sense of superiority instilled in her by her father. Growing up in a prominent family, she developed an inflated sense of pride that alienated her from the townspeople. This attitude contributed to her reluctance to accept help or support from others, reinforcing her isolation. Even when the townspeople attempted to address the unpleasant odor emanating from her property, they did so discreetly, reflecting their complex feelings toward Emily's plight.

The absence of healthy relationships in Emily's life left her vulnerable when she finally did meet someone—Homer Barron. Her desire for love and companionship clashed with the emotional scars left by her father's control. When Homer showed interest in her but later withdrew, Emily's fear of abandonment triggered a desperate response. She resorted to murder as a means of retaining control over the one person who had dared to enter her life.

Emily's behavior can be seen as a tragic consequence of her father's oppressive influence. The lack of autonomy she experienced throughout her formative years left her ill-equipped to navigate adult relationships or cope with loss in a healthy manner. Her actions were not merely those of a scorned lover but rather the culmination of years spent in emotional captivity.

Ultimately, Emily's relationship with Mr. Grierson shaped every aspect of her existence—from her inability to form connections with others to her misguided attempts at love. His overprotectiveness and domineering nature created a toxic environment that stifled Emily's growth and led to tragic outcomes in her later life.

In summary, Emily's relationship with her father was characterized by dominance and control, leading to emotional dependence and stunted personal growth. Mr. Grierson's actions prevented Emily from developing independence or appropriate social skills, resulting in profound isolation and an inability to cope with change or loss. This unhealthy dynamic left lasting scars that influenced Emily's behavior long after his death, culminating in tragic choices that reflected both desperation and despair.

How Emily's father's death affect her mental state

Emily's father's death had a profound and destabilizing effect on her mental state, plunging her into a deep psychological crisis. The relationship she shared with Mr. Grierson was characterized by control and dependency, leaving her ill-prepared to cope with life on her own. When he passed away, Emily found herself not only grieving the loss of her father but also grappling with the overwhelming reality of solitude.

Initially, Emily's reaction to her father's death was one of denial. For three days, she refused to acknowledge that he had died, keeping his body in their home. This behavior reflected her deep-seated inability to let go and her morbid attachment to him. The townspeople were concerned but also somewhat intrigued by her refusal to accept reality. Emily's denial served as a coping mechanism, shielding her from the emotional turmoil of facing life without the only person who had been a constant presence in her life.

The death of Mr. Grierson left Emily feeling utterly alone and destitute. With him gone, she lost not only a father but also her protector and the only source of emotional support she had ever known. The isolation she experienced during his life intensified after his death, as she had no social skills or relationships outside of their home. This lack of a support system exacerbated her feelings of loneliness, making it difficult for her to navigate the world without him.

Financially, Emily was left in a precarious position. With Mr. Grierson's death, she inherited nothing but the family home—an empty shell that echoed with memories of a life once filled with control and dominance. The townspeople began to pity her, seeing her as a relic of the past who had lost everything. This shift in perception added another layer of complexity to Emily's mental state; she was no longer the proud daughter of a prominent family but rather a woman on the brink of poverty and despair.

As time passed, Emily's mental health deteriorated further. The isolation that had been imposed upon her throughout her life became even more pronounced after her father's death. She became reclusive, rarely leaving the house and avoiding interactions with townspeople who had once looked upon her with reverence. Her physical appearance changed dramatically; she cut her hair short—a stark departure from societal norms—which signaled a break from the past and perhaps an internal struggle that was manifesting outwardly.

Emily's inability to cope with change was evident in how she interacted with others following her father's death. When Homer Barron entered her life, he briefly offered hope for companionship and love. However, Emily's past experiences left her emotionally unprepared for this new relationship. Her fear of abandonment—rooted in years spent under her father's control—led to obsessive behavior when it came to Homer. She clung to him desperately, fearing that he too would leave her.

The townspeople observed these changes with a mix of concern and judgment. They viewed Emily as an oddity—someone who had once commanded respect but now seemed lost in a world that had moved on without her. Their gossip reflected their discomfort with her mental state; they whispered about her eccentricities while simultaneously feeling pity for the woman they once admired.

Emily's mental decline culminated in tragic actions that further alienated her from society. After Homer disappeared from her life, presumably due to his fears about commitment, Emily resorted to desperate measures to maintain control over him. She purchased arsenic and ultimately killed him—a horrifying act born from years of emotional turmoil and fear of abandonment.

In summary, the death of Emily's father triggered a profound mental crisis that left her grappling with loneliness, denial, and an inability to cope with change. Her relationship with Mr. Grierson had fostered dependency and isolation, which only intensified after his passing. As Emily descended into madness, she became a tragic figure—a woman unable to let go of the past or embrace the future—ultimately leading to devastating consequences for herself and those around her.

How Emily's denial of her father's death impact her relationships with others

Emily's denial of her father's death significantly impacted her relationships with others, creating a complex web of isolation and misunderstanding. After Mr. Grierson's passing, Emily's refusal to accept the reality of his death left her in a state of emotional turmoil that alienated her from the community around her. For three days, she kept his body in their home, insisting to visitors that he was still alive. This denial not only showcased her inability to confront loss but also highlighted her deep-seated dependency on her father, which had stunted her emotional growth.

The townspeople, who had long viewed Emily as an obligation and a curiosity, were both concerned and perplexed by her behavior. Their attempts to reach out—offering condolences and support—were met with Emily's bizarre insistence that her father was not dead. This refusal to acknowledge reality created a barrier between her and the community, reinforcing their perception of her as an eccentric figure rather than a grieving daughter. Instead of fostering connections, her denial pushed people away, leaving her even more isolated.

Emily's relationship with her father had been one of control and overprotection, which left her ill-equipped to handle life on her own. His death stripped away the last vestiges of security she had known, plunging her into a world where she felt utterly alone. With no siblings or mother mentioned in the narrative, Emily's social network was virtually nonexistent. The townspeople had witnessed Mr. Grierson driving away potential suitors throughout Emily's life, effectively robbing her of any chance at forming meaningful relationships. Now that he was gone, she found herself without the emotional tools necessary to navigate a life devoid of his presence.

The impact of this isolation became evident as Emily began to withdraw further into herself. Her mental state deteriorated; she became reclusive and stopped engaging with the outside world altogether. The townspeople observed this change with a mix of pity and judgment, often gossiping about her odd behavior instead of offering genuine support. They treated Emily as an enigma rather than a person in need of compassion, further entrenching her sense of alienation.

Emily's relationship with Homer Barron marked another turning point in her life—a brief glimmer of hope amidst the darkness that enveloped her. However, even this relationship was tainted by the shadows of her past. Her fear of abandonment—rooted in years spent under her father's control—manifested in obsessive behavior towards Homer. When he began to withdraw from their relationship, Emily's inability to cope led to tragic consequences.

The townspeople's perception of Emily shifted dramatically after Mr. Grierson's death; they began to see her as a tragic figure rather than an object of scorn or curiosity. Yet their pity did little to alleviate her loneliness. Instead of reaching out to help Emily heal, they continued to whisper about her eccentricities while maintaining a safe distance. Their actions—such as secretly treating the odor emanating from her property—illustrated their complex feelings toward her; they felt responsible yet were unwilling to confront her directly.

Emily's denial also affected how she viewed herself in relation to others. Her father's oppressive nature instilled in her a sense of false pride and superiority that alienated potential friends and suitors alike. Even after his death, she clung to remnants of this identity, refusing to acknowledge the realities that surrounded her. The townspeople remembered how Mr. Grierson had chased away suitors and stifled any chance for Emily to engage socially; now they saw a woman trapped by the very legacy he had left behind.

When Emily finally allowed herself to face the reality of her father's death—after being forced by doctors and ministers—it marked a significant turning point in her mental state but did little to mend the rift between herself and the community. Instead of providing closure or healing, it further solidified her status as an outsider who could not adapt to change or loss.

In summary, Emily's denial of her father's death profoundly impacted her relationships with others by isolating her emotionally and socially. Her inability to confront reality created barriers that alienated potential friends and deepened existing divides with the townspeople who once felt obligated to support her. The legacy of control left by Mr. Grierson haunted Emily long after his death, shaping not only how she interacted with others but also how she viewed herself within the world—a tragic figure caught between past trauma and present despair.

How did Emily's denial of her father's death affect her interactions with the townspeople

Emily's denial of her father's death had a profound impact on her interactions with the townspeople, shaping their perceptions of her and altering the dynamics of their relationships. When Mr. Grierson passed away, Emily's refusal to acknowledge his death for three days became a spectacle for the community. The townspeople, who had long viewed her with a mix of curiosity and pity, were drawn into the drama of her denial. Instead of offering genuine support, they became spectators to her unraveling, which only deepened her isolation.

Initially, when the women of the town came to pay their respects, Emily insisted that her father was still alive. This bizarre charade left them bewildered and concerned but also somewhat hesitant to confront her directly. Their attempts to express sympathy were met with Emily's insistence on maintaining the facade, which created a barrier between her and the community. Rather than fostering connections, this denial pushed people away, reinforcing the perception that she was an eccentric figure unworthy of genuine engagement.

The townspeople were aware of Emily's codependent relationship with her father and understood that she had been emotionally stunted by years of isolation. They remembered how Mr. Grierson had driven away potential suitors, leaving Emily without any meaningful relationships. As a result, when she clung to his memory in denial, they felt a mix of pity and judgment. Their gossip about her behavior reflected their discomfort with her mental state rather than any desire to help.

Emily's refusal to accept reality also highlighted her inability to cope with loss, further alienating her from those around her. After finally yielding to pressure and allowing her father's body to be buried, she fell into a long period of reclusiveness. The townspeople noted that after his death—and after Homer Barron left—Emily was rarely seen outside her home. This withdrawal from society only intensified their perception of her as a tragic figure, someone who had once commanded respect but now seemed lost in a world that had moved on without her.

As time passed, Emily's interactions with the townspeople became increasingly strained. They observed her eccentricities with a mix of fascination and disdain; she became a subject of local gossip rather than a member of the community. The once-grand Grierson home fell into disrepair, mirroring Emily's own decline. The townspeople's pity was tinged with resentment as they watched someone who had once held herself above them now struggle with poverty and isolation.

Despite their awareness of Emily's struggles, the townspeople often chose to maintain their distance. Their pity did not translate into meaningful support; instead, it fostered an environment where Emily felt even more isolated. When complaints arose about the foul odor emanating from her home following Mr. Grierson's death, rather than confronting her directly, they resorted to discreetly sprinkling lime around her property in an attempt to mask the smell. This passive approach underscored their reluctance to engage with Emily on a human level.

Emily's refusal to engage with the community led to misunderstandings about her character and intentions. For instance, when she began dating Homer Barron—a man beneath her social status—the townspeople were scandalized. They viewed this relationship as a betrayal of family pride and tradition rather than an opportunity for Emily to find companionship after years of isolation. Their judgment further alienated her; instead of celebrating this newfound connection, they scrutinized it through the lens of social class and propriety.

When Homer disappeared from Emily's life, it marked another turning point in how she interacted with others. The townspeople speculated about what had happened between them but were too afraid or unwilling to confront Emily directly about it. This avoidance only deepened her sense of isolation; she became trapped in a cycle of loneliness that compounded after each failed relationship or interaction.

Ultimately, Emily's denial and subsequent reclusiveness culminated in tragic outcomes that shocked the community when they finally discovered the truth about her life after her death. The revelation that she had kept Homer's corpse in an upstairs room for years shattered any lingering notions they had about her being merely eccentric or tragic; it exposed the depths of her mental illness and despair.

In summary, Emily's denial of her father's death profoundly affected her interactions with the townspeople by deepening her isolation and transforming their perceptions of her from pitying observers to reluctant spectators in a tragic drama. Her inability to confront reality created barriers that alienated potential friends and deepened existing divides within the community. The combination of gossip, judgment, and passive avoidance left Emily trapped in a cycle of loneliness that ultimately led to devastating consequences for both herself and those around her.

CHAPTER 3

The long-term consequences of Emily's codependency with her father

Emily's codependency with her father had far-reaching long-term consequences that deeply affected her mental health, social interactions, and overall ability to navigate life independently. Growing up in a household dominated by Mr. Grierson's authoritarian presence, Emily was conditioned to rely heavily on him for emotional support and guidance. This dependency stunted her personal development and left her ill-prepared for the realities of adulthood.

One of the most significant impacts of this codependency was Emily's struggle with self-esteem. Her father's overprotectiveness instilled in her a sense of inadequacy; she learned to measure her worth based on his approval. This constant need for validation created a cycle of anxiety and low self-esteem that persisted throughout her life. When Mr. Grierson passed away, Emily found herself devoid of the only source of affirmation she had ever known, leading to a profound identity crisis.

The denial of her father's death further exacerbated these issues. For three days, Emily refused to acknowledge his passing, keeping his body in their home. This behavior was not merely an act of mourning but a manifestation of her inability to cope with loss and change. Her denial isolated her from the community, who were left bewildered by her actions. Instead of receiving support during this vulnerable time, Emily became a subject of gossip and pity, reinforcing her feelings of alienation.

Emily's interactions with the townspeople became strained as a result of her father's death and her subsequent denial. The community had long viewed her as an obligation—someone to be observed from a distance rather than engaged with meaningfully. After Mr. Grierson's death, their pity transformed into a mix of concern and judgment, further alienating Emily at a time when she needed connection the most.

The lack of social skills developed during her years under her father's control made it difficult for Emily to form healthy relationships. She had been shielded from potential suitors and meaningful friendships, leaving her ill-equipped to navigate adult interactions. When Homer Barron entered her life, he briefly offered hope for companionship; however, Emily's fear of abandonment—rooted in her upbringing—led to obsessive behavior that ultimately pushed him away.

Emily's mental health deteriorated further as she retreated into isolation following her father's death. The vibrant social life she might have cultivated was replaced by a reclusive existence marked by loneliness and despair. The townspeople watched as she became increasingly disconnected from reality, reinforcing their perception of her as an eccentric figure rather than someone in need of help.

In addition to social isolation, Emily's financial situation worsened after Mr. Grierson's death. Left with nothing but the family home—a decaying relic of the past—she struggled to maintain even basic living conditions. This financial instability compounded her feelings of helplessness and despair, making it difficult for her to assert any independence in a world that felt increasingly hostile.

As time passed without resolution or closure regarding Homer's fate, Emily's mental state continued to decline. Her inability to confront reality led to tragic outcomes; she resorted to murder as a means of retaining control over Homer when she feared losing him just as she had lost her father. This act was not merely about love but rather an expression of desperation rooted in years of emotional turmoil.

The long-term consequences of Emily's codependency with her father ultimately manifested in tragic ways that underscored the complexity of human relationships shaped by control and dependency. Her inability to cope with loss, combined with a lack of social skills and emotional support systems, left Emily trapped in a cycle of isolation and despair that culminated in devastating choices.

In summary, Emily's codependency with her father led to long-term consequences that severely impacted her mental health and relationships with others. The combination of low self-esteem, social isolation, financial instability, and an inability to cope with change created a perfect storm that ultimately defined the tragic trajectory of her life after Mr. Grierson's death.

How Emily's codependency with her father affect her independence

Emily's codependency with her father had a profound impact on her independence, shaping her ability to function as an autonomous individual in society. Throughout her life, Mr. Grierson's overprotective nature and authoritarian control stifled Emily's growth, leaving her ill-equipped to navigate the complexities of adult life once he was gone.

From a young age, Emily was conditioned to rely on her father for emotional support and decision-making. Mr. Grierson's belief that no man was good enough for his daughter led him to drive away potential suitors, effectively isolating Emily from forming meaningful relationships. This isolation fostered a deep dependency on him, as he became not just her protector but also the sole source of validation and identity in her life. As a result, Emily struggled to develop her sense of self-worth and independence.

When Mr. Grierson died, Emily found herself unprepared for the realities of life without him. Her immediate reaction was one of denial; she kept his body in their home for three days, unable to confront the loss and the implications it had for her future. This denial was a manifestation of her codependency, as she clung to the remnants of their relationship rather than accepting the need to forge her own path. The townspeople observed this behavior with a mix of pity and concern, but their attempts to reach out were met with Emily's insistence that her father was still alive.

The death of Mr. Grierson left Emily in a precarious position—emotionally and financially. With no skills or experience outside the confines of her father's control, she struggled to assert herself in a world that had changed dramatically. The home that once provided security became a prison, reinforcing her isolation and inability to engage with others. The townspeople watched as she retreated further into solitude, which only deepened their perception of her as an eccentric figure.

Emily's lack of independence became evident in her interactions with the community. When approached by officials regarding taxes or other matters, she responded by referencing Colonel Sartoris—an outdated figure who had exempted her family from taxes long ago—demonstrating her disconnect from reality and inability to adapt to changing circumstances. This reliance on past arrangements highlighted how deeply entrenched she was in the legacy of her father's control.

As time passed, Emily's mental health deteriorated further due to her inability to cope with loss and change. The isolation imposed by her codependent relationship with Mr. Grierson left her without the emotional tools necessary to navigate adult relationships or handle grief effectively. When Homer Barron entered her life, he represented a fleeting opportunity for connection; however, Emily's fear of abandonment led to obsessive behavior that ultimately drove him away.

The tragic culmination of Emily's codependency was evident when she resorted to murder as a means of retaining control over Homer after he disappeared from her life. This act was not merely about love but rather an expression of desperation rooted in years of emotional turmoil and fear of being alone. It underscored how deeply intertwined her sense of self was with those she depended on—first with her father and later with Homer.

In summary, Emily's codependency with her father severely impacted her independence by stifling personal growth and leaving her ill-prepared for adult life after his death. Her inability to confront loss, compounded by social isolation and mental health struggles, resulted in tragic outcomes that defined the course of her life. Ultimately, Emily became a prisoner of her past—a woman unable to break free from the chains of dependency that had bound her since childhood.

After the long-term consequences of Emily's codependency with her father, her life began to unfold in ways that were both challenging and transformative. The death of Mr. Grierson left her grappling with a profound sense of loss, but it also opened the door for her to confront the emotional turmoil that had long been buried beneath layers of denial and dependency.

In the weeks following her father's funeral, Emily found herself ensnared in a thick fog of grief. The initial shock gradually morphed into a suffocating denial that enveloped her thoughts and actions. She clung to the remnants of her father's presence, keeping his belongings untouched and refusing to engage with the reality of his absence. This denial was not merely an act of mourning; it became a silent battlefield where she fought against the tide of sorrow threatening to engulf her.

As days turned into weeks, Emily's mental state began to unravel. The vibrant tapestry of her social life unraveled thread by thread, leaving her ensnared in a monochrome world devoid of joy and connection. Each day spent in isolation spared her from facing the piercing gaze of pity from the townspeople but also sowed seeds of alienation within her. Relationships atrophied under the weight of unshared grief, and Emily grappled with the duality of seeking solace in solitude while mourning the loss of connection.

In this desolate landscape, Emily's mental health began to reveal its fragility. The energy she expended on obsessive behaviors reflected a profound inner turmoil seeking an outlet—a way to vocalize the silent scream of grief that had found no other expression. This period marked a critical juncture in her grieving process, allowing her to confront the rawest facets of her pain.

Gradually, Emily began to explore the roots of her grief. She realized that her father's control had shaped not only her identity but also her sense of safety and belonging in the world. This exploration laid bare the necessity of rebuilding that sense from within rather than seeking it solely from external sources. Through this challenging phase, she started to internalize the strength and guidance she once sought from Mr. Grierson, learning how to provide it for herself in his absence.

As time passed, Emily's denial began to shift into acceptance. She started recognizing that clinging to her father's memory would not bring him back nor restore the life they once shared. This realization marked a subtle yet significant shift toward healing—wherein she began weaving together the fragmented pieces of her past and present into a tapestry that honored her father's memory while embracing her capacity for resilience and growth.

Emily's interactions with the townspeople shifted as well. Initially met with pity and judgment, she slowly began to reclaim her narrative. The gossip surrounding her life transformed from whispers about her eccentricities to discussions about her strength in facing adversity. The townspeople saw glimpses of change as she ventured outside more frequently, engaging in conversations and attempting to rebuild connections that had frayed during her years of isolation.

The arrival of Homer Barron marked another turning point in Emily's life—a chance for companionship that she had long been denied. Their relationship provided a temporary escape from loneliness, igniting feelings she had suppressed for so long. However, old patterns emerged as Emily grappled with fear and insecurity rooted in her past experiences with men.

While Homer initially showed interest in Emily, his eventual withdrawal triggered deep-seated fears related to abandonment. Instead of fostering healthy communication, Emily's anxiety manifested in obsessive behaviors as she struggled to maintain control over this new relationship. Her past experiences with Mr. Grierson resurfaced, causing emotional turmoil as she oscillated between hope and despair.

Despite these challenges, Emily continued to evolve through therapy and self-reflection. She learned valuable coping strategies for managing anxiety and low self-esteem while fostering resilience through new experiences. Engaging in activities that brought joy—such as painting or gardening—allowed Emily to reclaim parts of herself that had been lost during years spent under her father's control.

As she navigated these changes, Emily found solace in community involvement. Volunteering at local events helped bridge gaps between herself and others while fostering connections built on shared interests rather than dependency or obligation. This newfound sense of purpose provided an anchor amid emotional upheaval.

Over time, Emily's relationship with Homer became more complex as she sought balance between love and independence. While he represented a chance at happiness, she recognized that true fulfillment could not come from another person alone; it required self-acceptance and internal strength cultivated through healing.

The turning point came when Emily confronted Homer about their future together—a conversation filled with vulnerability where she expressed both love and fear. This moment marked a departure from old patterns; instead of clinging desperately out of fear, she chose honesty as a means for connection—a significant shift toward emotional maturity.

As weeks turned into months, Emily continued to embrace change while honoring memories tied to both her father and Homer Barron. She learned how grief could coexist with joy—how loss could shape identity without defining it entirely. This realization allowed for deeper healing as she forged ahead on a path toward self-discovery.

Eventually, Emily found herself standing at a crossroads—one where choices lay before her like open doors leading into uncharted territory filled with possibilities yet unseen. With each step taken toward independence came renewed confidence; no longer was she defined solely by past relationships but rather empowered by them as part of an intricate tapestry woven over time.

In embracing vulnerability while cultivating resilience through community engagement and personal exploration, Emily discovered newfound freedom within herself—a liberation from old patterns that had once held sway over every aspect of life—from love to identity itself.

The journey was not without its challenges; moments of doubt still surfaced occasionally like shadows lurking just beyond reach—but now they were met with strength rather than despair—a testament to how far she had come since those early days spent grappling with loss alone behind closed doors.

As seasons changed outside—the world continued turning unabated by personal struggles—Emily stood poised ready for whatever lay ahead; no longer trapped within confines imposed by others but rather stepping boldly into each new day filled with promise hope laughter love all intertwined beautifully along this remarkable path called life!

CHAPTER 4

Emily's sense of identity changed after her father's death

After her father's death, Emily Grierson experienced a profound transformation in her sense of identity, marked by a complex interplay of grief, denial, and the struggle for autonomy. Initially, Emily's identity was inextricably linked to her father; he was not only her protector but also the sole source of validation and emotional security. With his passing, she faced the daunting task of reconstructing her identity in a world that felt suddenly unfamiliar.

In the immediate aftermath of Mr. Grierson's death, Emily's reaction was one of denial. She kept his body in their home for three days, refusing to accept the reality of his absence. This denial served as a defense mechanism, shielding her from the overwhelming grief that threatened to engulf her. By clinging to the remnants of her father's presence, Emily attempted to maintain a sense of stability in an otherwise chaotic emotional landscape.

As she navigated this period of denial, Emily's sense of self began to fracture. Her identity had been so closely tied to her father's authority that she struggled to envision a life without him. The townspeople observed this transformation with a mix of pity and judgment, seeing her as both a relic of the past and a figure trapped in her own psychological turmoil. Their whispers reflected their discomfort with her decline, further isolating Emily at a time when she needed connection the most.

In grappling with her grief, Emily began to explore the roots of her dependency on her father. This exploration laid bare the foundational impact he had on her sense of safety and belonging in the world. As she confronted these feelings, she realized that she needed to rebuild that sense from within rather than seeking it solely from external sources or memories of her father.

The isolation that followed Mr. Grierson's death sowed seeds of alienation within Emily. Each day spent alone was a day spared from facing the piercing gaze of pity or awkward condolences from others. However, this very isolation also unraveled the vibrant tapestry of her social life. Relationships withered under the weight of unshared grief and silence, leaving Emily ensnared in a monochrome world devoid of joy and connection.

Emily's mental state teetered between stagnation and evolution as she grappled with the duality of seeking solace in solitude while mourning the loss of connection. The absence of her father forced her to confront uncomfortable truths about herself—truths that had long been obscured by his overbearing presence.

As time passed, Emily began to internalize the strength and guidance she once sought from her father. This marked a subtle yet significant shift toward healing; she started weaving together the fragmented pieces of her past and present into a tapestry that honored his memory while embracing her capacity for resilience and growth. The process was neither linear nor easy; it involved moments of regression as well as breakthroughs.

Emily's interactions with the townspeople began to shift as well. Initially met with pity and judgment, she slowly started reclaiming her narrative. The gossip surrounding her life transformed from whispers about eccentricities to discussions about strength in facing adversity. As she ventured outside more frequently and engaged in conversations, glimpses of change emerged.

The arrival of Homer Barron marked another turning point for Emily—a chance for companionship that had long been denied to her. Their relationship ignited feelings she had suppressed for years but also brought forth old patterns rooted in fear and insecurity. As she grappled with these emotions, Emily recognized that true fulfillment could not come solely from another person; it required self-acceptance cultivated through healing.

Despite these challenges, Emily continued to evolve through therapy and self-reflection. She learned valuable coping strategies for managing anxiety while fostering resilience through new experiences. Engaging in activities that brought joy—such as painting or gardening—allowed Emily to reclaim parts of herself lost during years spent under her father's control.

As she navigated these changes, Emily found solace in community involvement. Volunteering at local events helped bridge gaps between herself and others while fostering connections built on shared interests rather than dependency or obligation. This newfound sense of purpose provided an anchor amid emotional upheaval.

Over time, Emily's relationship with Homer became more complex as she sought balance between love and independence. While he represented a chance at happiness, she recognized that true fulfillment could not come from another person alone; it required self-acceptance nurtured through healing.

The turning point came when Emily confronted Homer about their future together—a conversation filled with vulnerability where she expressed both love and fear. This moment marked a departure from old patterns; instead of clinging desperately out of fear, she chose honesty as a means for connection—a significant shift toward emotional maturity.

As weeks turned into months, Emily continued embracing change while honoring memories tied to both her father and Homer Barron. She learned how grief could coexist with joy—how loss could shape identity without defining it entirely. This realization allowed for deeper healing as she forged ahead on a path toward self-discovery.

Eventually, Emily found herself standing at a crossroads—one where choices lay before her like open doors leading into uncharted territory filled with possibilities yet unseen. With each step taken toward independence came renewed confidence; no longer was she defined solely by past relationships but rather empowered by them as part of an intricate tapestry woven over time.

In embracing vulnerability while cultivating resilience through community engagement and personal exploration, Emily discovered newfound freedom within herself—a liberation from old patterns that had once held sway over every aspect of life—from love to identity itself.

The journey was not without its challenges; moments of doubt still surfaced occasionally like shadows lurking just beyond reach—but now they were met with strength rather than despair—a testament to how far she had come since those early days spent grappling with loss alone behind closed doors.

As seasons changed outside—the world continued turning unabated by personal struggles—Emily stood poised ready for whatever lay ahead; no longer trapped within confines imposed by others but rather stepping boldly into each new day filled with promise hope laughter love all intertwined beautifully along this remarkable path called life!

CHAPTER 5

How Emily's grief manifests in her daily life

Emily's grief after her father's death manifested in various ways, deeply affecting her daily life and interactions with others. Initially, she entered a state of denial that was both profound and unsettling. For three days, she kept her father's body in their home, refusing to acknowledge his death. This behavior indicated not just a refusal to confront reality but also highlighted the depth of her codependency; she could not let go of the only source of emotional security she had ever known.

During this time, Emily's home became a mausoleum—filled with memories and remnants of her father's life. The very act of keeping his body nearby served as a coping mechanism, allowing her to cling to the illusion that he was still present. This denial created a thick layer of emotional insulation, shielding her from the pain of loss while simultaneously barricading her from moving through the grieving process.

As days turned into weeks, Emily's initial shock morphed into a heavy cloak of denial that enveloped her thoughts and actions. Conversations about her father were met with mechanical diversions to safer topics; memories were locked away in the deepest recesses of her mind, surfacing only as fleeting shadows quickly banished by the light of denial. This stage exemplified the human psyche's capacity for self-preservation, yet it underscored the delicate balance between avoiding pain and confronting reality.

The townspeople observed Emily's behavior with a mix of concern and judgment. Their attempts to offer condolences were met with her insistence that her father was still alive. This reaction not only alienated them but also reinforced Emily's isolation. She became an object of curiosity rather than a person in need of support, further deepening her sense of loneliness.

Emily's grief also manifested in obsessive behaviors that reflected her inner turmoil. The energy expended on these compulsive rituals served as an outlet for her unexpressed emotions—a way to vocalize the silent scream of grief that had found no other expression. These obsessive acts became markers on her path toward acceptance and recovery, indicating both pain endured and progress made.

As she grappled with these compulsions, Emily unknowingly laid down stepping stones across the turbulent waters of mourning. Each obsessive act represented a struggle against the tide of sorrow threatening to engulf her. In this liminal space between denial and acceptance, she began to confront the rawest facets of her pain—allowing herself to experience vulnerability rather than retreating into emotional isolation.

The phase of regression into childlike dependency was another critical juncture in Emily's grieving process. By allowing herself to experience this longing for protection, she engaged in an essential exploration of grief's roots. This exploration laid bare the foundational impact her father had on her sense of safety and belonging in the world. It highlighted the necessity of rebuilding that sense from within rather than seeking it solely from external sources.

As Emily navigated this challenging phase, she started to internalize the strength and guidance she once sought from her father. This marked a subtle yet significant shift toward healing—wherein she began weaving together fragmented pieces of her past and present into a tapestry that honored his memory while embracing her capacity for resilience and growth.

Her daily interactions began to reflect these changes as well. Initially met with pity and judgment by the townspeople, Emily slowly started reclaiming her narrative. The gossip surrounding her life transformed from whispers about eccentricities to discussions about strength in facing adversity. As she ventured outside more frequently and engaged in conversations, glimpses of change emerged.

The arrival of Homer Barron marked another turning point for Emily—a chance for companionship that had long been denied to her. Their relationship ignited feelings she had suppressed for years but also brought forth old patterns rooted in fear and insecurity. As she grappled with these emotions, Emily recognized that true fulfillment could not come solely from another person; it required self-acceptance cultivated through healing.

Despite these challenges, Emily continued to evolve through therapy and self-reflection. She learned valuable coping strategies for managing anxiety while fostering resilience through new experiences. Engaging in activities that brought joy—such as painting or gardening—allowed Emily to reclaim parts of herself lost during years spent under her father's control.

As time passed, Emily's relationship with Homer became increasingly complex as she sought balance between love and independence. While he represented a chance at happiness, she recognized that true fulfillment could not come from another person alone; it required self-acceptance nurtured through healing.

The turning point came when Emily confronted Homer about their future together—a conversation filled with vulnerability where she expressed both love and fear. This moment marked a departure from old patterns; instead of clinging desperately out of fear, she chose honesty as a means for connection—a significant shift toward emotional maturity.

As weeks turned into months, Emily continued embracing change while honoring memories tied to both her father and Homer Barron. She learned how grief could coexist with joy—how loss could shape identity without defining it entirely. This realization allowed for deeper healing as she forged ahead on a path toward self-discovery.

Eventually, Emily found herself standing at a crossroads—one where choices lay before her like open doors leading into uncharted territory filled with possibilities yet unseen. With each step taken toward independence came renewed confidence; no longer was she defined solely by past relationships but rather empowered by them as part of an intricate tapestry woven over time.

In embracing vulnerability while cultivating resilience through community engagement and personal exploration, Emily discovered newfound freedom within herself—a liberation from old patterns that had once held sway over every aspect of life—from love to identity itself.

The journey was not without its challenges; moments of doubt still surfaced occasionally like shadows lurking just beyond reach—but now they were met with strength rather than despair—a testament to how far she had come since those early days spent grappling with loss alone behind closed doors.

As seasons changed outside—the world continued turning unabated by personal struggles—Emily stood poised ready for whatever lay ahead; no longer trapped within confines imposed by others but rather stepping boldly into each new day filled with promise hope laughter love all intertwined beautifully along this remarkable path called life!

CHAPTER 6

Emily stepped onto the train, her heart racing with a mix of excitement and apprehension. The rhythmic clatter of the wheels against the tracks echoed her thoughts as she settled into her seat by the window. Outside, the world blurred into a tapestry of greens and browns, a stark contrast to the hectic life she was leaving behind. She had decided to take this trip to Chicago not just for the adventure, but to escape the weight of her responsibilities, if only for a little while. The train's departure marked a new beginning, a chance to breathe and rediscover herself amidst the chaos that had become her everyday life.

As the train picked up speed, Emily found herself lost in thought until an unexpected voice broke her reverie. "Mind if I sit here?" A tall, charming man stood before her, his smile warm and inviting. Ryan had an air of confidence about her, with tousled hair and an easy demeanor that instantly put her at ease. She nodded, gesturing to the empty seat across from her. This spontaneous encounter felt serendipitous; perhaps it was fate that had brought them together on this journey.

Their conversation began with small talk, casual exchanges about their destinations and favorite travel experiences. Emily learned that Ryan was an avid traveler, having explored various corners of the world. His stories were captivating, filled with humor and vivid details that made her laugh. In turn, she shared snippets of her life back home, carefully omitting the stressors that had driven her to seek refuge in Chicago. As they spoke, Emily felt a connection forming, one that transcended mere acquaintance; it was as if they had known each other for much longer than just a few minutes.

As the train rolled into Chicago, the skyline emerged in the distance, a breathtaking view that took Emily's breath away. The towering buildings glimmered under the afternoon sun, each one telling its own story of ambition and dreams. Ryan suggested they explore the city together before their evening plans, and Emily found herself agreeing without hesitation. The prospect of wandering through the vibrant streets with someone as intriguing as Ryan filled her with anticipation.

Stepping off the train, they were greeted by a bustling atmosphere, street performers entertaining passersby and food vendors offering tantalizing aromas that wafted through the air. They strolled along Michigan Avenue, marveling at the architecture and indulging in spontaneous detours to quaint shops and art galleries. With each shared laugh and playful banter, Emily felt her worries begin to dissolve; she was simply enjoying the moment.

As dusk began to settle over the city, Ryan suggested they find a place for dinner. He had done some research on romantic restaurants in

Chicago and mentioned one that had received rave reviews: Mon Ami Gabi. Intrigued by his choice, Emily agreed wholeheartedly. The thought of sharing a meal in such an intimate setting added an exciting layer to their burgeoning connection.

Arriving at Mon Ami Gabi, they were enveloped in an ambiance of warmth and charm. The dimly lit restaurant exuded romance with its rustic decor and soft music playing in the background. They were seated at a cozy table by the window with a view of the bustling street outside, a perfect spot for people-watching while enjoying their meal together.

As they perused the menu filled with French delicacies, their conversation flowed effortlessly from topic to topic—travel dreams, favorite books, and even childhood memories. Over glasses of wine and delectable dishes like steak frites and escargot, Vera felt as though she was discovering not just Ryan but also parts of herself that had been neglected for too long.

The evening unfolded like a beautiful dream; laughter mingled with clinking glasses as they toasted to new beginnings. With every shared bite and glance across the table, Emily realized how rare it was to connect with someone so effortlessly. As they finished their meal, Ryan proposed dessert—a rich chocolate mousse that promised to be as sweet as their evening together.

With hearts full and spirits lifted, Emily and Ryan stepped back into the cool Chicago night. The city lights sparkled like stars above them as they walked side by side down tree-lined streets. In that moment, surrounded by laughter and warmth, Emily knew this was just the beginning of something special—an unexpected journey marked by connection and possibility.

CHAPTER 7

As they strolled through the lively streets of Chicago, Ryan began to share tales from his travels that captivated Emily's imagination. He spoke of backpacking through the lush landscapes of New Zealand, where he had hiked the Tongariro Alpine Crossing, a breathtaking trek that left him in awe of nature's beauty. His eyes sparkled with enthusiasm as he recounted encounters with locals, the thrill of bungee jumping, and the serenity of starry nights spent camping under the vast sky. Each story painted vivid pictures in Emily's mind, allowing her to escape into a world filled with adventure and wonder.

Ryan then shifted gears and shared a more humorous tale from his time in Italy. He described a cooking class he had taken in a small Tuscan village, where he accidentally set off the smoke alarm while trying to flambé a dish. The image of him flailing about as the instructor rushed to his aid made Emily laugh heartily. "I think I'll stick to eating Italian rather than cooking it," he chuckled, and Emily couldn't help but agree. These lighthearted moments drew them closer, bridging the gap between two strangers who had just met.

As their evening continued, Emily felt a twinge of guilt creeping in. While she was enjoying this unexpected connection with Ryan, her mind drifted back to her responsibilities waiting for her at home. Her job as a marketing manager often consumed her thoughts, even during moments meant for relaxation. She struggled to find a balance between work and leisure, feeling torn between her professional obligations and the newfound joy she experienced with Ryan.

"Are you okay?" Ryan asked gently, noticing her sudden shift in demeanor. Emily hesitated before admitting her internal conflict. She shared how difficult it was for her to disconnect from work, even when she was physically away from it. Ryan listened intently, nodding in understanding. "It's hard to let go sometimes," he said thoughtfully. "But life is too short not to enjoy these moments." His words resonated deeply with her, igniting a flicker of hope that perhaps she could find a way to embrace both worlds.

As they moved on from dinner and found themselves at a nearby café for dessert, the atmosphere shifted back to lightheartedness. They shared stories about their childhoods—Ryan's mischievous adventures growing up in a small town contrasted with Emily's more reserved upbringing in the city. They laughed over silly incidents that had shaped them into who they were today—like Ryan's infamous prank involving a rubber chicken at his high school graduation or Emily's embarrassing moment when she tripped on stage during a school play.

Their laughter echoed through the café, drawing curious glances from other patrons. It was refreshing for Emily to let go of her worries and simply enjoy the moment. Each chuckle brought them closer together, creating an invisible thread that intertwined their lives for this brief encounter. The ease with which they connected felt magical; it was as if they were two puzzle pieces fitting perfectly together.

Later that night, after finishing their desserts, they wandered to a quiet park nearby where they could see the stars twinkling above them like diamonds scattered across black velvet. The city lights faded into the background as they settled onto a bench beneath an old oak tree. The cool breeze carried whispers of secrets as they began to talk about deeper topics—dreams, fears, and what truly mattered in life.

Emily opened up about her struggles with self-doubt and the pressure she felt to succeed professionally while maintaining personal happiness. Ryan shared his own vulnerabilities—his fear of settling down too soon and losing his sense of adventure. Their midnight conversations flowed effortlessly under the starry sky, each revelation drawing them closer together as they explored their hopes for the future.

The vulnerability shared between them created an intimate bond that felt rare and precious. In that moment, time seemed to stand still;

all that mattered was their connection under the vast expanse of stars—a reminder that amidst life's chaos, there were still moments of clarity and understanding waiting to be discovered.

The next morning arrived with anticipation as they boarded the train once again, this time heading toward the majestic Rocky Mountains. The rhythmic sound of the train wheels against the tracks felt comforting after their night of deep conversations and laughter. As they settled into their seats by the window, Emily couldn't help but feel excited about what lay ahead.

As the train chugged along, they watched as flat plains transformed into rolling hills before giving way to towering peaks cloaked in snow-capped glory. Each passing landscape seemed more breathtaking than the last; Emily found herself captivated by nature's beauty outside their window while Ryan pointed out various landmarks along the way.

"Look at that!" Ryan exclaimed as they crossed into Colorado, where mountains loomed larger than life against the clear blue sky. The air felt different here—crisper and filled with promise—and Emily felt invigorated by it. They spent hours chatting animatedly about everything from their favorite outdoor activities to bucket list adventures while soaking in stunning views.

As they approached a particularly scenic overlook where mountains met sky in an explosion of color, Emily felt an overwhelming sense of gratitude wash over her. This trip had already changed her perspective on life; it reminded her that sometimes stepping away from routine allowed space for new experiences and connections.

With each mile traveled through this magnificent landscape, Emily realized how much she had needed this journey—physically and emotionally. She glanced at Ryan beside her; his enthusiasm was infectious and made every moment feel alive with possibility.

As they ventured deeper into the heart of the Rockies, Emily knew this adventure was just beginning—a chapter filled with exploration and connection waiting to unfold before them like an open road leading into uncharted territory.

CHAPTER 8

As the train wound its way through the Rocky Mountains, Emily and Ryan were treated to breathtaking views that seemed to change with every passing moment. The landscape unfolded like a grand tapestry, with towering pines and rugged cliffs juxtaposed against the serene blue of the sky. Each time the train slowed for a scenic stop, they eagerly hopped off to stretch their legs and soak in the beauty around them.

At one particular stop, they disembarked at a small wooden platform nestled among the trees. The air was crisp and invigorating, filled with the scent of pine and fresh earth. Emily took a deep breath, feeling as though she were inhaling pure freedom. They wandered along a nearby trail that led to a stunning overlook, where they could see the valley below blanketed in vibrant wildflowers. Ryan pulled out his phone to capture the moment, encouraging Emily to pose with the mountains as her backdrop.

"Let's make this our first travel selfie together!" he said with a playful grin. Emily laughed and struck a pose, her heart fluttering at the thought of this spontaneous adventure. As Ryan snapped the photo, she felt a rush of joy at how effortlessly they connected—two souls exploring not just a new place but also each other's company.

LOVE IN TRANSIT 47

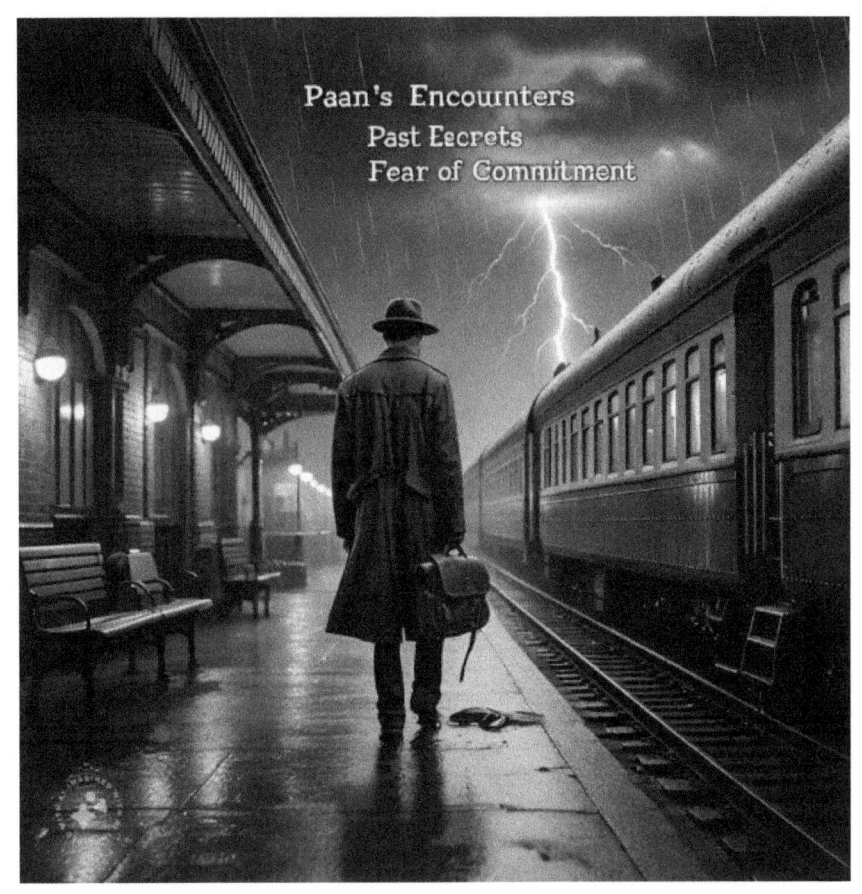

Paan's Encounters
Past Eecrets
Fear of Commitment

After their photo session, they sat on a large rock at the edge of the overlook, taking in the view in comfortable silence. The sound of birds chirping and leaves rustling in the gentle breeze created a serene atmosphere that allowed them to reflect on their journey thus far. "I can't believe how much we've done in such a short time," Emily mused, glancing at Ryan. "It feels like we've known each other for ages."

Ryan nodded thoughtfully. "It's amazing how travel can create connections so quickly. It strips away all the distractions and lets you focus on what really matters." His words resonated deeply with Emily; she felt as if this trip was not just an escape but also an opportunity for personal growth.

Back on the train, they resumed their journey through the Rockies, but this time with an eagerness to explore local culture as well. Ryan suggested they research some small towns along their route where they could stop for lunch and experience authentic mountain cuisine. Emily loved the idea—this was exactly what she had hoped for when embarking on this adventure.

After some quick research on their phones, they decided to stop in Estes Park, known for its quaint charm and proximity to Rocky Mountain National Park. As they arrived, Emily felt a sense of excitement bubbling within her. The town was picturesque, with rustic buildings adorned with colorful flowers and welcoming storefronts that beckoned them inside.

They wandered through local shops filled with handmade crafts and artisanal goods. Emily marveled at a collection of handcrafted jewelry made from stones sourced from nearby mountains while Ryan picked up some locally roasted coffee beans as a souvenir. "I'll need these for my next adventure," he joked, holding up the bag as if it were a trophy.

For lunch, they chose a cozy café that boasted farm-to-table dishes featuring ingredients sourced from local farms. As they settled into their seats, Emily felt invigorated by the atmosphere—the warm wooden interior and friendly chatter of fellow diners created an inviting ambiance that made her feel at home.

Over plates of hearty sandwiches and fresh salads, they exchanged stories about their favorite foods from around the world. Ryan recounted his love for street food in Southeast Asia while Emily shared her fondness for homemade pasta from her grandmother's kitchen. Their laughter filled the café as they playfully debated which cuisine was superior—a lighthearted competition that only deepened their bond.

After lunch, they ventured into Rocky Mountain National Park to immerse themselves in nature's embrace fully. The air was crisp and refreshing as they hiked along one of the park's many trails that wound through towering pines and vibrant wildflowers. With each step, Emily felt more alive; nature had a way of grounding her while simultaneously lifting her spirits.

As they trekked deeper into the woods, Ryan pointed out various plants and wildlife along their path—the delicate petals of columbine flowers swaying gently in the breeze and squirrels darting playfully between trees. He had an infectious enthusiasm for nature that made every detail seem fascinating.

"Did you know that these mountains are home to elk?" he asked excitedly while gesturing toward a distant ridge where he believed they might be spotted later in the day. Emily smiled at his enthusiasm; it was refreshing to see someone so passionate about their surroundings.

Eventually, they reached a serene lake nestled among the mountains—a hidden gem that sparkled under the afternoon sun. The water mirrored the surrounding peaks perfectly, creating an idyllic scene straight out of a postcard. They found a quiet spot by the shore where they could sit and soak it all in.

As they sat side by side on a large rock overlooking the lake, Ryan pulled out his phone again to take more pictures—this time capturing candid moments of laughter between them as they attempted to skip stones across the water's surface. Each splash echoed like music against nature's backdrop, reminding them both of how simple joys often brought about profound happiness.

As dusk began to settle over the mountains, painting the sky in hues of orange and pink, Emily suggested they find a spot to watch the sunset before heading back to town. Ryan readily agreed; he had been hoping for just such an opportunity to share this moment with her.

They hiked back toward an elevated viewpoint that Ryan had mentioned earlier—a place he had discovered during previous visits to Estes Park. When they arrived at the overlook just in time for sunset, Emily was speechless; before them lay an expansive view of rolling hills bathed in golden light.

As the sun dipped below the horizon, casting long shadows over the landscape, Emily felt overwhelmed by beauty—the kind that tugged at her heartstrings and reminded her how precious life could be when one took time to appreciate it fully.

"Wow," she breathed softly as she leaned against Ryan's shoulder, feeling both comforted and exhilarated by his presence beside her. He wrapped an arm around her shoulders instinctively; it felt natural—a gesture that spoke volumes without needing words.

They sat together in silence as twilight enveloped them like a warm blanket; stars began twinkling overhead one by one until it seemed like an entire universe had come alive above their heads. In that moment of stillness under countless stars shining brightly against an indigo sky, Emily realized how deeply she had connected with Ryan—not just as fellow travelers but as kindred spirits navigating life's journey together.

The following morning brought renewed energy as they prepared to leave Estes Park behind and continue their adventure through Colorado's stunning landscapes. The train ride ahead promised more breathtaking views—an exhilarating journey into uncharted territory filled with possibilities waiting just beyond each bend.

As they boarded once again—this time feeling more like companions than strangers—Emily glanced out at the scenery unfolding outside her window: majestic peaks rising high above valleys below while rivers wound gracefully through canyons carved over millennia by nature's hand.

With every mile traveled together on this train journey across America's heartland came new experiences that would forever shape who they were becoming—not only individually but also collectively as friends bonded by shared laughter and moments etched into memory forevermore.

Ryan turned toward her mid-journey with an expression filled with sincerity: "I'm really glad we met on this trip." His words resonated deeply within her; she felt grateful for every twist of fate that had led them here together amidst these breathtaking landscapes.

"Me too," Emily replied earnestly—her heart swelling with emotion as she realized how transformative this journey had been thus far—not just because of its scenic beauty but because it had opened her eyes to new perspectives about herself and what truly mattered most in life.

As they continued onward into Colorado's vast wilderness—eagerly anticipating whatever lay ahead—Emily knew one thing for certain: this chapter was only just beginning—a story woven together through friendship forged amidst nature's splendor waiting patiently ahead on tracks leading them toward endless possibilities yet unseen.

CHAPTER 9

As the train continued its journey through the breathtaking Rocky Mountains, Emily and Ryan found themselves nestled in a cozy corner of their compartment, the rhythmic sound of the train soothing their spirits. The beauty of the landscape outside was mesmerizing, but it was the emotional landscape within that began to take center stage. They had shared laughter, adventure, and moments of joy, but now it was time to confront the fears that lingered beneath the surface.

"Can we talk about what happens next?" Emily asked, her voice barely above a whisper. Ryan turned to her, sensing the weight of her words. He nodded, his expression serious yet encouraging. "Of course. What's on your mind?"

LOVE IN TRANSIT

Emily took a deep breath, gathering her thoughts. "I've had such an incredible time with you, but I can't shake this feeling of uncertainty. What if this connection we've built is just temporary? What if we go back to our lives and lose touch?" Her vulnerability hung in the air, palpable and raw.

Ryan reached for her hand, intertwining his fingers with hers. "I've been thinking about that too," he confessed. "It's easy to get swept away in the moment and forget about reality. But I don't want to lose what we have." His gaze held hers with sincerity, and Emily felt a flicker of hope igniting within her.

"I'm scared," she admitted, her voice trembling slightly. "Scared of opening my heart again after everything I've been through." Ryan squeezed her hand reassuringly. "You're not alone in this. I have my fears too—about commitment, about being vulnerable. But I believe in what we're building together."

Their conversation deepened as they shared their insecurities—Ryan spoke of his fear of settling down too quickly and losing his sense of adventure, while Emily opened up about her struggle with balancing work and personal life. They realized that both of them had been running from their fears rather than confronting them head-on.

As they spoke openly about their hopes and dreams for the future, Emily felt a sense of relief wash over her. It was liberating to share these burdens with someone who understood her struggles. Their heart-to-heart conversation solidified their bond further, transforming uncertainty into a shared commitment to navigate whatever lay ahead together.

With their hearts laid bare and fears confronted, Emily and Ryan began to envision a future together—a future filled with possibilities that extended beyond this trip. As they continued their journey through the mountains, they brainstormed ideas for how they could maintain their connection once they returned to their respective lives.

"What if we set a date to meet again?" Ryan suggested, his eyes sparkling with excitement. "We could explore another city together or even plan a weekend getaway." The thought thrilled Emily; it was a tangible way to keep the momentum going between them.

"I love that idea!" she exclaimed, feeling a surge of enthusiasm. "Maybe we could visit Denver or even head back to Chicago for a second round of adventures." They spent the next hour discussing potential destinations and activities—hiking trails they wanted to explore, restaurants they wanted to try, and experiences they wanted to share.

As they mapped out potential plans on Ryan's phone, Emily felt a sense of purpose blossoming within her. This trip had reignited her passion for life beyond work; it reminded her that adventure could be found not just in travel but also in relationships.

"Let's make it official," Ryan proposed playfully as he held out his pinky finger. "Pinky promise that we'll make this happen." Emily laughed at his earnestness but took his hand in hers nonetheless. "Pinky promise," she echoed, sealing their commitment with a smile.

With each passing moment on the train, Emily felt more certain about what lay ahead; this was not just a fleeting romance but the beginning of something meaningful—a partnership built on trust and shared experiences.

As the train approached its final destination—Denver—the atmosphere inside their compartment shifted from anticipation to bittersweet nostalgia. They had spent so much time together over these past few days that saying goodbye felt daunting despite the excitement of new beginnings ahead.

Ryan leaned back in his seat, gazing out at the sprawling cityscape coming into view. "I can't believe our adventure is almost over," he said softly, almost as if he were trying to hold onto every last moment before it slipped away.

Emily nodded in agreement; she felt a mix of sadness and gratitude for all they had experienced together—the laughter shared over meals, the quiet moments spent under starlit skies, and the heart-to-heart conversations that had deepened their connection.

As the train rolled into Denver's bustling station, they gathered their belongings with reluctance. The vibrant energy of the city was palpable as passengers disembarked around them; yet for Emily and Ryan, it felt like stepping into an unknown world without each other by their sides.

"Let's take one last picture before we leave," Ryan suggested with a smile that masked his own apprehension about parting ways. They posed together against the backdrop of the train station—a snapshot capturing not just their faces but also the memories forged during this unforgettable journey.

After taking several photos and laughing at each other's silly poses, reality began to sink in: this was it—the moment they would have to say goodbye for now.

Standing on the platform amid bustling travelers readying themselves for new adventures felt surreal; everything seemed alive around them while their hearts felt heavy with impending separation.

"I guess this is it," Emily said quietly as she looked up at Ryan—his expression mirroring her own mix of sadness and hopefulness.

"I'll miss you," he replied earnestly, brushing a strand of hair behind her ear—a tender gesture that sent shivers down her spine.

"I'll miss you too," she admitted softly; tears threatened to spill from her eyes despite her efforts to stay composed. They embraced tightly as if trying to merge into one another—holding onto each other for dear life before stepping into uncertainty alone once more.

"Promise me you'll text me when you get home?" Ryan asked as he pulled back slightly but kept his hands resting on her shoulders—his touch grounding amidst swirling emotions around them.

"Of course," Emily promised through a shaky breath; she knew she would cherish every message exchanged until they could be together again.

With one last lingering look filled with unspoken words between them—words that conveyed how much this journey meant—their hands reluctantly slipped apart as reality set in: they were heading back into separate lives once more.

Days turned into weeks after their bittersweet goodbye at Denver's train station; both Emily and Ryan returned home filled with memories yet grappling with an undeniable void left by each other's absence. They exchanged texts often—sharing snippets of daily life while reminiscing about moments spent together during their trip—but nothing compared to being side by side.

One evening while scrolling through photos from their adventure together on her phone—each image evoking laughter or warmth—Emily felt an overwhelming urge rise within her; she couldn't ignore it any longer—she needed to see him again.

Gathering her courage like never before, she picked up her phone and sent Ryan a message: "What do you think about meeting up next weekend? I can't stop thinking about our adventure."

To her delight—and relief—within minutes came his enthusiastic response: "Absolutely! Let's plan something fun!"

They spent hours discussing options until finally deciding on an impromptu weekend trip back to Chicago—a city filled with memories waiting patiently for them both.

On Friday evening as Emily boarded the train once more—this time heading toward Ryan—her heart raced with anticipation; she couldn't wait to reunite with him after weeks apart filled only by texts and longing glances at shared photos.

When she arrived at Union Station in Chicago—the familiar sights igniting feelings reminiscent of their first meeting—she spotted him waiting eagerly near arrivals; his face lit up upon seeing her—a sight that made all those weeks apart worth every moment endured alone.

"Emily!" he exclaimed joyfully as he rushed forward wrapping his arms around her tightly; warmth enveloped them both as if no distance had ever separated them at all—their hearts beating in sync once more amidst bustling crowds around them.

"I missed you so much!" she breathed against his shoulder feeling tears prick at her eyes—not from sadness but pure joy radiating through every fiber within herself knowing they were finally together again where they belonged—side by side embarking on another adventure filled with love waiting patiently ahead on tracks leading toward endless possibilities yet unseen.

CHAPTER 10
EPILOGUE

As the seasons changed and the months rolled on, Emily and Ryan found themselves navigating the complexities of a relationship that had blossomed from a chance encounter on a train. Their journey together was not just about the places they visited but also about the emotional landscapes they traversed—filled with laughter, vulnerability, and the occasional uncertainty. Each moment spent together was a reminder of how travel had brought them together, allowing them to forge a bond that felt both exhilarating and grounded.

The power of travel to unite people became evident as they explored new cities together, each trip serving as a backdrop for their growing connection. From bustling markets in New Orleans to serene beaches in California, every adventure added layers to their relationship. They learned to embrace spontaneity, often deciding on their next destination over breakfast or even while packing for a weekend getaway. This sense of adventure kept their relationship fresh and exciting, reminding them that life was meant to be lived fully in the moment.

However, with every beautiful sunrise came the shadows of their pasts—Emily's lingering fears of heartbreak and Ryan's apprehension about commitment. They had both faced their share of disappointments, which made them cautious about fully opening their hearts again. Yet, through countless conversations under starry skies and quiet moments shared over cups of coffee, they began to dismantle those walls. Emily learned that vulnerability was not a weakness but a strength, while Ryan discovered that embracing love did not mean losing his sense of self.

Balancing work and personal life became another theme in their journey together. Emily's role as a marketing manager often demanded long hours and intense focus, while Ryan continued his travels for work. They made it a priority to communicate openly about their schedules, ensuring that neither felt neglected or overwhelmed by the demands of their careers. Weekends became sacred; they would plan mini-adventures or cozy nights in, making the most of their time together despite their busy lives.

As they navigated these challenges, Emily found herself reflecting on her past relationships—how fear had often dictated her choices and held her back from pursuing happiness. With Ryan, she felt empowered to confront those fears head-on. She realized that love was not about perfection but about embracing imperfections together. The fear of heartbreak no longer loomed over her like a dark cloud; instead, it transformed into an opportunity for growth and deeper connection.

Ryan also found himself evolving through this relationship. He had always been a free spirit, hesitant to settle down for fear of losing his adventurous lifestyle. However, with Emily by his side, he discovered that love could coexist with adventure. They began to plan trips that combined both—hiking in national parks during the day and stargazing at night, creating memories that intertwined their passions for exploration and connection.

One evening, as they sat on the balcony of their rented cabin overlooking a serene lake, Ryan turned to Emily with a thoughtful expression. "You know," he began slowly, "I never thought I'd find someone who understands my need for adventure while also being my home." His words resonated deeply within her; she felt seen and cherished in ways she hadn't experienced before.

Emily smiled softly, feeling warmth spread through her chest. "I feel the same way," she admitted. "You've shown me that it's okay to take risks—both in love and in life." In that moment, they both understood that they were no longer just two travelers passing through each other's lives; they were partners committed to exploring the journey ahead together.

As they continued to build their lives side by side, Emily and Ryan made plans not just for future trips but for a future together—a shared vision filled with love, laughter, and endless adventures. They talked about dreams of living abroad for a year or starting a travel blog to document their experiences. It was exhilarating to think about what lay ahead—a world filled with possibilities waiting to be explored.

Months later, as they stood at the train station once more—this time ready to embark on another journey together—they exchanged knowing smiles filled with excitement and anticipation. The train would take them to yet another destination, but more importantly, it symbolized their commitment to one another—a promise that no matter where life took them, they would face it together.

"Forever in transit," Ryan said with a grin as he took her hand firmly in his. Emily laughed lightly at his words but felt the truth behind them resonate deeply within her heart. They were indeed forever in transit—not just across landscapes but through life itself—embracing every moment as it came while cherishing the love they had found amidst the chaos of travel.

With hearts full of hope and excitement for what lay ahead, Emily and Ryan boarded the train hand in hand—ready for whatever adventures awaited them on this beautiful journey called life.

Don't miss out!

Visit the website below and you can sign up to receive emails whenever Pag-yel Taglan Rutherford publishes a new book. There's no charge and no obligation.

https://books2read.com/r/B-A-KCUEB-UZLDF

BOOKS 2 READ

Connecting independent readers to independent writers.

Did you love *Love In Transit*? Then you should read *The Journey of A Revert Muslim*[1] by Pag-yel Taglan Rutherford!

In the recent world of Islam, trying to establish and walk on a path to building a better faith as a Muslim can be more frustrating, especially for those who are new to Islam (The Reverts).

"THE JOURNEY OF A REVERTED MUSLIM" serves as a comprehensive companion for individuals accepting Islam as their way of life. This book offers a thoughtful roadmap through the complexes of Islamic practice, culture, and spirituality.

From the basics of belief and prayer to shaping social interactions and community engagement, this guide addresses the practicalities and nuances of living as a Muslim in today's world. With clarity and compassion, it explores fundamental concepts such as the five pillars of

---

1. https://books2read.com/u/mgYV1v

2. https://books2read.com/u/mgYV1v

Islam, the importance of character development, and the significance of community support.

In addition to covering essential topics like Islamic ethics, family life, and the Quranic teachings, "THE JOURNEY OF REVERTED MUSLIM" delves into the rich history and diverse traditions of Islam, providing context and depth to the reader's path of discovery. Through personal anecdotes, practical advice, and spiritual insights, this book empowers new Muslims to navigate their faith with confidence and grace.

Whether you are a recent convert, a curious seeker, or a supportive friend or family member, "THE JOURNEY OF REVERTED MUSLIM" offers invaluable guidance and inspiration for embracing Islam with sincerity, humility, and a steadfas

t heart.

Read more at taglanrutherfordpagyel@gmail.com.

Also by Pag-yel Taglan Rutherford

The Journey of A Revert Muslim
Boundaries For A Balanced Life
Love In Transit
Love In Transit
Moonlight On The Mississippi

Watch for more at taglanrutherfordpagyel@gmail.com.

About the Author

I am a versatile freelancer with a diverse skill set that encompasses content writing, Non-fiction writing, and teaching in subjects like Chemistry and Mathematics. With experience as a tutorial master and Calculus tutor. I excel in educational roles while also offering services in fitness, freight trade, translation and Data entry. My background in sales and marketing further enhances my ability to create compelling content and engage audiences effectively.

Read more at taglanrutherfordpagyel@gmail.com.